A Box of Friends

By **Pam Muñoz Ryan**
Illustrated by **Mary Whyte**

GINGHAM DOG
P R E S S

Columbus, Ohio

Children's Publishing

Text © 2003 Pam Muñoz Ryan
Illustrations © 2003 Mary Whyte
Cover Illustrations © 2003 Mary Whyte

This edition published in the United States of America in 2003 by
Gingham Dog Press,
an imprint of McGraw-Hill Children's Publishing,
a Division of The McGraw-Hill Companies
8787 Orion Place
Columbus, Ohio 43240-4027

www.MHkids.com

Library of Congress Cataloging-in-Publication Data is on file with the publisher.

Printed in The United States.

1-57768-420-6

1 2 3 4 5 6 7 8 9 10 PHXBK 09 08 07 06 05 04 03

Annie lived with her parents and her grandmother in a new house, in a new town, where almost nothing seemed familiar. Not the smooth sandy beach. Not the palm trees that rustled in the wind. Not even the sea gulls that seemed to always call her name, "An-nee! An-nee!"

Go away, she thought. *Leave me alone.*

The back porch was crowded with things that someone had left behind—colored bottles, rinsed-out cans, and weathered spoons. Annie examined a small blue bottle that looked as if it had passed through many hands.

This is someone else's house, she thought. *I don't belong here. I belong in the other house with the big climbing tree, the sidewalks for bike-riding, and my school around the corner.*

"Do you need some help unpacking?" asked Grandma.

Annie hadn't even unpacked the boxes in her room because she didn't want to stay.

A tear streamed down her face.

"I don't have any friends here," she said.

Grandma smiled. "When I was your age, I was just like you, quiet and shy. But I learned that everyone has a box of friends that they can take with them wherever they go."

"I don't," said Annie.

"Would you like to see mine?" said Grandma.

Annie followed Grandma upstairs, wondering where someone would keep a box of friends. *How could a person fit in a box? Was it a big box or a little box? Was it heavy or light?*

They went into Grandma's room. She had already unpacked, and it looked as if she had lived in it for many years.

Grandma reached into her closet and pulled out a box with a lid wrapped in fancy paper.

They sat on the bed, and Grandma slowly took off the cover.

Annie peeked inside. There was nothing but odds and ends. A gray feather. A smooth, round stone, white as shoe polish. A bouquet of dried roses. A small piece of driftwood, dotted with tiny holes.

Puzzled, Annie said, "There are no friends inside."

Grandma held up the gray feather. "Margaret is one of my friends. We used to be neighbors and loved to go shopping. Once, we bought matching hats with gray feathers on top. This is the feather that was on my hat. We still talk on the phone, write letters, and tell each other our deepest secrets."

Grandma picked up the smooth, round stone, white as shoe polish. "Your grandpa gave me this stone before he died. One day, he found it in the woods and brought it home to me, grinning like a schoolboy. He said it reminded him of our love, round and never-ending. Did you know that I was his best friend?"

Annie remembered her best friends and the memories that were still packed away.

"What about these?" said Annie, holding up the bouquet of roses, dried and faded pink.

"My sister and I made this together. When we were younger, we used to collect wildflowers and make bouquets, then hang them upside-down to dry. We used to argue all the time, fighting like cats and dogs. But even after all that bickering, we're still good friends."

Grandma lifted out the driftwood, dotted with tiny holes. "I found this at the beach the other day while I was taking a long walk by myself. I was thinking how lucky I am to be here in this new house with you and your mom and dad. So I gave it to myself as a present from me."

Annie had never heard of giving yourself a present.

"I want to make a box of friends," said Annie.

"I thought you would," said Grandma, already
pulling a shoebox out of her closet.

Annie chose fancy paper, striped like peppermints. She wrapped the
lid with it.

They went to Annie's room. Grandma sat in the wicker rocker
while Annie searched through her things until she found an arrowhead.

"I went to the mountains last summer with Matthew," said
Annie. "We ate banana and peanut butter sandwiches and played tag.
We looked for arrowheads, but I couldn't find one. Matthew found this
one and gave it to me."

Grandma smiled.

Annie put the arrowhead, shiny and black, into the box.

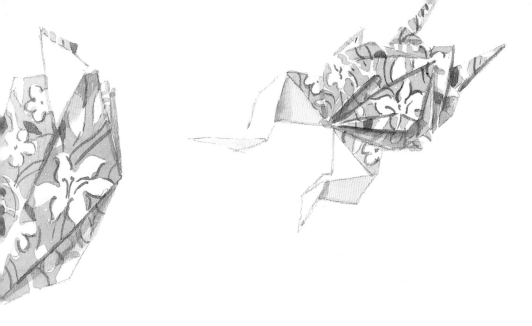

"And this?" said Grandma, picking up a paper frog, creased into sharp angles from green-flowered paper.

"That's my origami frog from my pen pal, Mika, in Japan," said Annie. "We've been writing to each other for two years."

"My, how far it has traveled," said Grandma. "She made this especially for you, took it to the post office, and mailed it all the way here?"

Annie nodded and put the paper frog, creased and flowered, into the box.

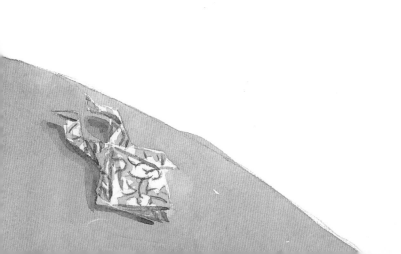

Annie held up a piece of a bone, hard and yellowed and encrusted with dirt. "Here's a bone Buster brought me," she said, petting Buster's head.

Grandma studied the bone. "It took a lot of digging to get this bone from the ground. Dogs love bones. That's a special kind of friend, someone who thinks of you first and is always loyal."

Annie hugged Buster. Grandma was right. Buster was as loyal as sunshine.

The bone went into the box.

Grandma picked up a packet of marigold seeds with a picture on the front that promised orange-burst flowers.

"Tyler and I bought those on the day we went on the school field trip to the nursery," said Annie. "I didn't have enough money, so he paid half and I gave him half the seeds."

Grandma said, "I'll bet he'll be your friend until those marigolds bloom a dozen times. He doesn't live that far away from here. You should invite him for a visit sometime."

Annie put the seed packet, with the promise of flowers, into the box.

Maybe she would invite Tyler for a visit, and Matthew, too, she thought.

Annie carried her box with her for the next few days. She saved a tiny abandoned bird's nest, woven with dried vines, to remind her of Papa because he brought it to her one morning. She saved a scrap of fabric to remind her of Mama, who was making Annie a dress from the same material.

She put the blue bottle in the box too, the one that had been left on the back porch and looked like it had passed through many hands. *It's for me*, she thought, and it made her smile to give it to herself.

Annie and Grandma went for a walk on the
beach. The waves licked at their bare feet and the
breeze tickled their cheeks. Annie found a shell,
hard and wavy on one side, and smooth and pink
on the other. She ran to show Grandma.

"That's lovely!" said Grandma.

"It's for you," said Annie. "To put in your box
of friends, from me."

"And this is for you," said Grandma, holding a
piece of green sea glass, rounded from the
pounding waves.

On the way back from the beach, Grandma checked the mail.

"Something came for you," she said, handing an envelope to Annie.

"It's an invitation to a party from a girl who lives down the road. I met her when she visited with her mother."

She must have liked me, thought Annie.

"And look at this. It says that you can bring a friend to the party," said Grandma.

That evening, Annie sat on the porch and studied the invitation. She wanted to go, but she was worried. How many kids would be at the party? Would they all be her age? Did some of them go to her new school? Would she have anyone to talk to?

The invitation did say that she could bring a friend.

Annie put the invitation into the box and looked out over the smooth sand and listened to the familiar sounds of the palm trees rustling in the wind and the sea gulls calling her name, "An-nee! An-nee!"

She hugged the box to her chest. *Who will I take to the party?* she wondered. Then she opened the box of friends and chose . . .

a piece of green sea glass,
rounded by the
pounding waves.